Mrs Christmas

Penny Ives

PUFFIN BOOKS

Last Christmas there was a near calamity. One morning in late December, Father Christmas woke up and found that he felt quite ill.

"Just look at you!" cried Mrs Christmas. "You're all covered in spots. How ever will I finish making all these presents by myself?"

"I'd better hurry up and feed the reindeer," Mrs Christmas said to herself.

But when she went into the stable she could hardly believe her eyes. The *reindeer* were covered in spots too! She decided to give them a dose of medicine while she considered what to do next.

First she put on her winter coat and went outside with her pet birds. Hundreds of letters to Father Christmas had fallen with the snow during the night. Together they gathered them all up.

Mrs Christmas read every letter. Then she rolled up her sleeves. Still so many toys to finish, even though she and Father Christmas had been working hard all year – ever since last Christmas in fact!

All day Mrs Christmas sawed and sewed and glued until everything was done.

But then she had a worrying thought. Without the reindeer how would she deliver the toys?

Whoopee! She suddenly had a
brilliant idea. She would
turn her bicycle into a
flying machine!

The vacuum cleaner would power her take-off! She
searched high and low in the cupboard for everything else
that she needed.

She fixed the vacuum so that
it would blow air out instead
of sucking it in.

Carefully she linked the pedals to
the motor. The faster she pedalled,
the faster it would go.

At last! The flying machine was ready! Mrs Christmas felt
very pleased with herself!

Mrs Christmas labelled each of the presents and stowed them away in her basket. One or two were rather large and proved to be quite troublesome!

Finally she put on her red suit and hat. No one would recognise her now!

Outside it was very cold. Mrs Christmas cleared a small runway in the snow ready for take-off.

The goose and the chicken flapped their wings hard and she pedalled furiously.

Round and round and round spun the wheels until the machine lifted silently into the air.

Mrs Christmas was flying!

Further and further flew Mrs Christmas until she saw a small town. She guided the bicycle in to land on a snowy rooftop.

Tying a long rope around the chimney, she lowered herself down.

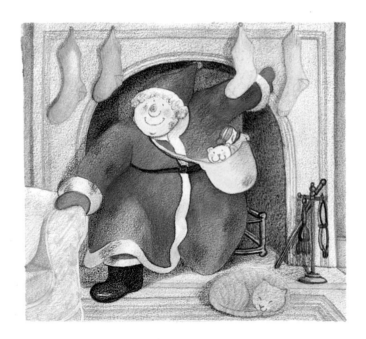

There! She had soot all over her lovely red suit. How did Father Christmas seem to keep so clean?

Mrs Christmas went up and down chimneys all night until
the very last present had been delivered and her baskets
were empty. Now she must make the journey home.

It seemed such a very long way. Suddenly
Mrs Christmas spotted a faint glow of lights.

It was Father Christmas and the reindeer guiding
her in to land!

They must be better! All their spots had gone! "I'm so glad you're home safely," said Father Christmas. "Come and sit down, dear, and take your boots off. I'll go and run you a lovely hot bath."

Mrs Christmas enjoyed a long, hot soak. When she felt better she went downstairs where there was a wonderful surprise waiting for her. . . .

Father Christmas had made a special breakfast with presents for everyone!

Happy Christmas!

PUFFIN BOOKS

Published by the Penguin Group
Penguin Books Ltd, 80 Strand, London WC2R 0RL, England
Penguin Group (USA) Inc., 375 Hudson Street, New York, New York 10014, USA
Penguin Group (Canada), 10 Alcorn Avenue, Toronto, Ontario,
Canada M4V 3B2 (a division of Pearson Penguin Canada Inc.)
Penguin Ireland, 25 St Stephen's Green, Dublin 2,
Ireland (a division of Penguin Books Ltd)
Penguin Group (Australia), 250 Camberwell Road,
Camberwell, Victoria 3124, Australia (a division of Pearson Australia Group Pty Ltd)
Penguin Books India Pvt Ltd, 11 Community Centre, Panchsheel Park, New Delhi – 110 017, India
Penguin Group (NZ), cnr Airborne and Rosedale Roads, Albany,
Auckland 1310, New Zealand (a division of Pearson New Zealand Ltd)
Penguin Books (South Africa) (Pty) Ltd, 24 Sturdee Avenue, Rosebank, Johannesburg 2196, South Africa

Penguin Books Ltd, Registered Offices: 80 Strand, London WC2R 0RL, England

www.penguin.com

First published by Hamish Hamilton Ltd 1990
Published in Picture Puffins 1992
Reissued in this edition 2005
9 10 8

Copyright © Penny Ives, 1990
All rights reserved

The moral right of the author/illustrator has been asserted

Manufactured in China

British Library Cataloguing in Publication Data
A CIP catalogue record for this book is available from the British Library

ISBN-13: 978-0-14055-434-2
ISBN-10: 0-140-55434-3